**M.P. ROBERTSON** is an internationally acclaimed
picture book author and illustrator, whose books include
*The Great Dragon Rescue, The Dragon Snatcher,*
*The Dragon and the Gruesome Twosome, Hieronymous Betts*
*and his Unusual Pets, Big Brave Brian, The Sandcastle,*
*Big Foot* and *Food Chain.*
He lives in Bradford-on-Avon, near Bath, with his partner,
the illustrator Sophy Williams, and their two sons.

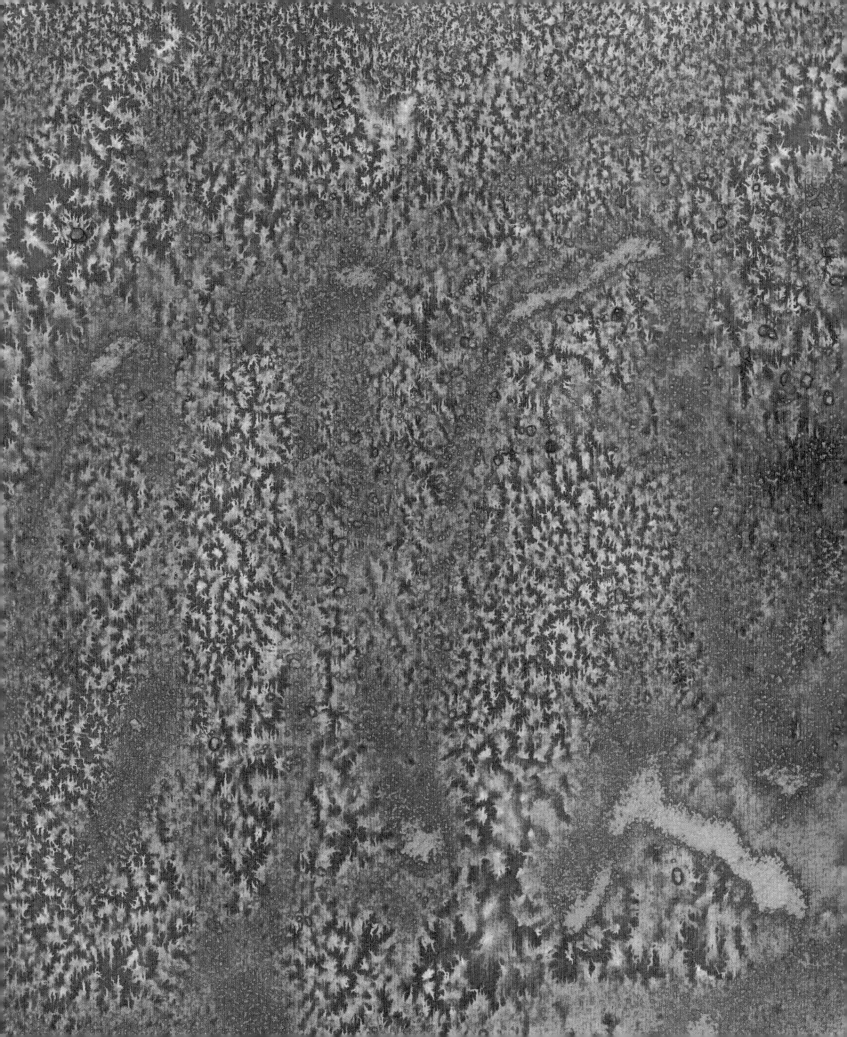

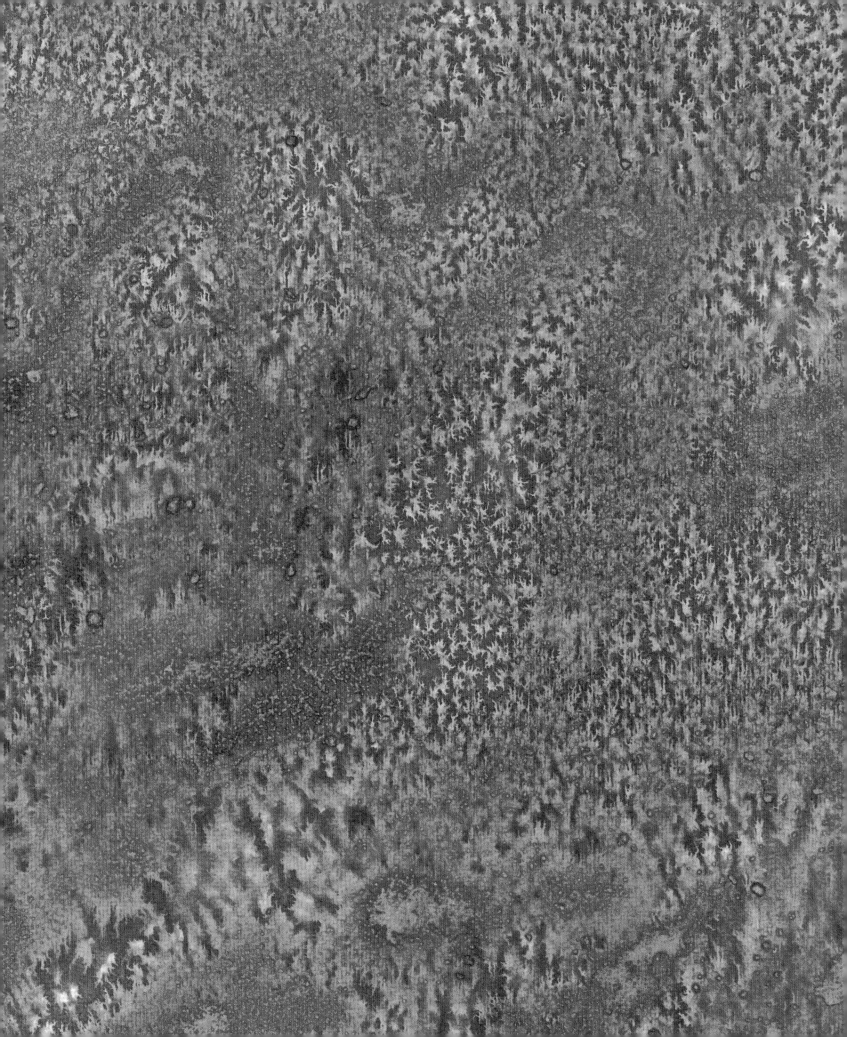

For Osky Bosky Boy (Oscar) – *M.P.R.*

*The Egg* copyright © Frances Lincoln Limited 2000
Text and illustrations copyright © M.P. Robertson 2000

First published in Great Britain in 2000 by
Frances Lincoln Children's Books, 4 Torriano Mews,
Torriano Avenue, London NW5 2RZ
www.franceslincoln.com

This paperback edition published in 2007

British Library Cataloguing in Publication Data available on request

ISBN 978-1-84507-799-0

Printed in China

3 5 7 9 8 6 4

# The
# EGG

## M.P. Robertson

**F**

FRANCES LINCOLN
CHILDREN'S BOOKS

G eorge knew something wasn't right, when he found more than he had bargained for under his mother's favourite chicken.

He moved the egg to the warmth
of his bedroom. For three days
and three nights he read the egg stories.

On the third night, the egg started to rumble.

Something was hatching, and it definitely wasn't a chicken …

When the dragon saw George, it gave a chirrup of delight.

George didn't speak Dragon, but he knew exactly what the dragon had said ...
"Mummy."

George had never been a mother before, but he knew that it was his motherly duty to teach the dragon dragony ways.

The first lesson he taught was *The Fine Art of Flying.*

The second lesson was *Fire and How to Breathe It.*

The third lesson was *How to Distress a Damsel*.

And the final lesson was *How to Duff a Knight*.

Every evening, as all good mothers should, George read the dragon a bedtime story.

One night, as he read from a book of dragon tales, the dragon looked longingly at the pictures. A sizzling tear rolled down his scaly cheek.

The dragon was lonely. He was missing his own kind.

The next morning, the dragon had gone.
George was very sad. He thought he
would never see his dragon again.

But seven nights later, he was woken
by the beating of wings. Excitedly, he
pulled back the curtains. There, perched in
the tree, was the dragon. George opened
the window and clambered onto his back.

They soared into the night, chasing the moon around the world, over oceans and mountains and cities.

Faster and faster they went, until they came to a place that was neither North nor South, East nor West.

They swooped down through
the clouds, into a cave that gaped
like a dragon's jaws. This was the
place where dragons lived.
   The dragon gave a roar
of delight. He was home at last.

Finally, it was time for George to leave.
Up, up they flew, chasing sleep through the night,
until they could see his home below.

George hugged his dragon tight,
and the dragon gave a roar. George
didn't speak Dragon, but he knew
exactly what the dragon had said …

… "Thank you."

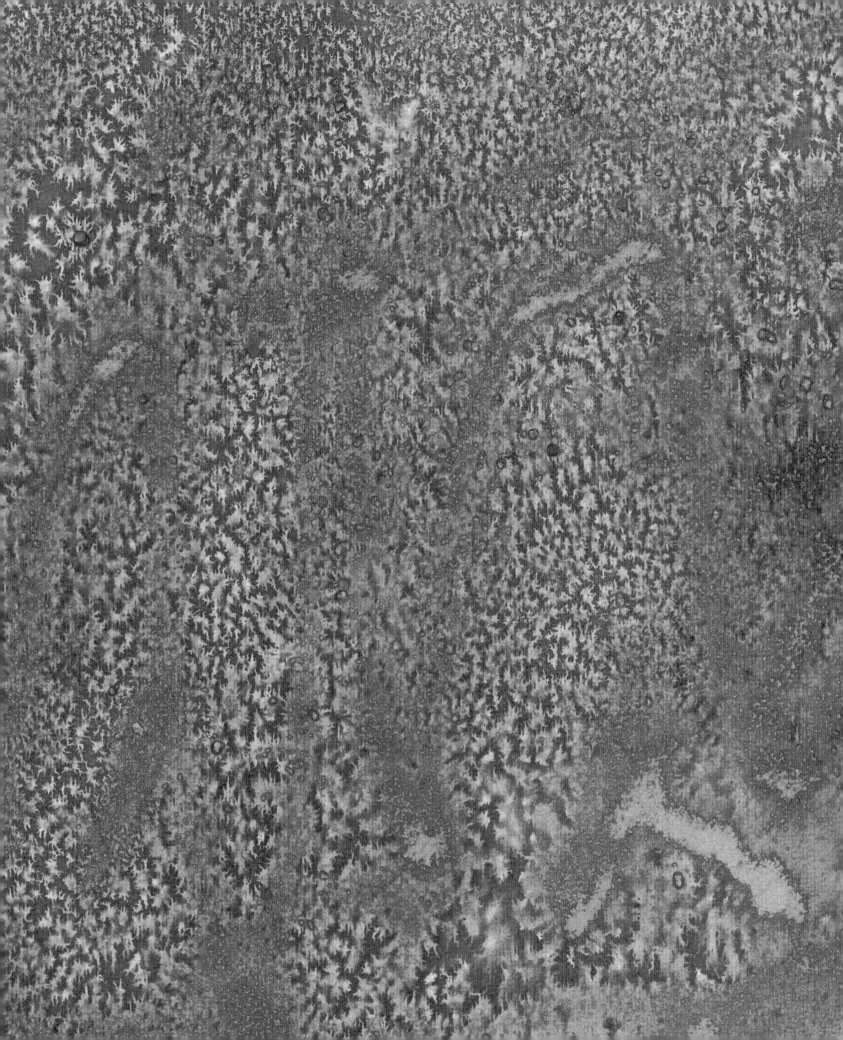

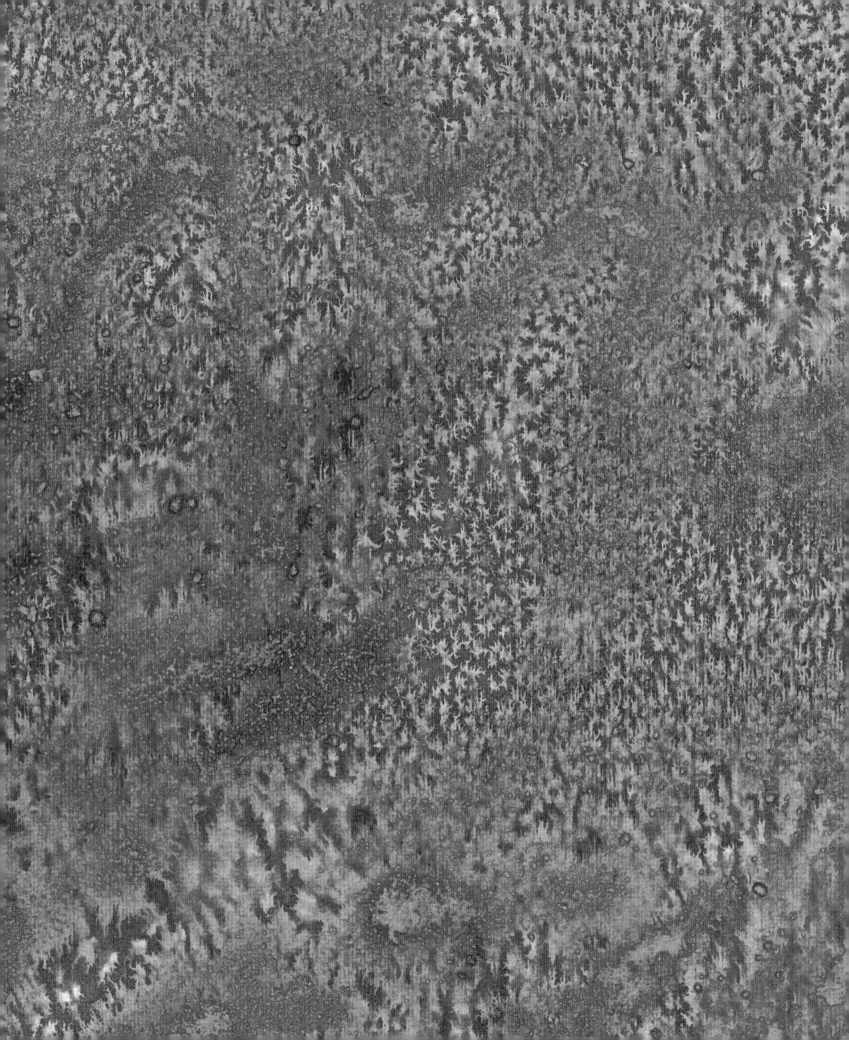

# MORE TITLES BY M.P. ROBERTSON FROM FRANCES LINCOLN CHILDREN'S BOOKS

## The Sandcastle

Jack loves building sandcastles more than anything in the world.
But he can't stop the sea from stealing them away. Then one day
he finds a shell with magical powers and makes a wish to be
king of his own sandcastle…

## Hieronymus Betts and his Unusual Pets

Hieronymus Betts has some very unusual pets. But he knows
of something that is slimier, noisier, greedier, scarier and stranger
than all of them put together. What on earth could it be?
Dare you read this book to find out?

## The Great Dragon Rescue

When George's dragon swoops out of the sky and carries him
off to a magical land, George knows an adventure has begun.
So when he meets a witch who has imprisoned a baby dragon,
George thinks up a clever scheme to rescue the baby and
reunite it with its dragon dad.

Frances Lincoln titles are available from all good bookshops.
You can also buy books and find out more about your favourite titles,
authors and illustrators on our website: www.franceslincoln.com